Gay Romance

a Sailor for Every Port

Chris Johns

WARNING

This book contains sexually explicit scenes and adult language. It may be considered offensive to some readers. This book is for sale to adults ONLY.

Please store your files wisely where they cannot be accessed by underage readers.

* * * * * * * * * * * * * * * * * * *

WANT FREE COPIES OF MY BOOKS?

Just visit my blog and download free copies of my books:

http://chris-johns.awesomeauthors.org/

About the Publisher

4Fun Publishing, a member of **BLVNP Incorporated**, 340 S. Lemon #6200, Walnut CA 91789, info@blvnp.com / legal@blvnp.com

NOTE: Due to the highly emotional reaction of some people to works of erotic fiction, any email sent to the above address that contains foul language or religious references is automatically deleted by our anti-spam software and will not be seen. All other communications are welcome.

DISCLAIMER

A Sailor for Every Port

Gay Romance

By: Chris Johns

ISBN: 978-1-62761-061-2

Part 1

I Join Up

I made it. Against the odds I had persuaded my parents to sign the papers and I was in. I had wanted it since I was eighteen but being a brilliant student had nearly sunk me.

I suppose I had better start at the beginning instead of talking in riddles.

Johnny Johnson was in my year at Grammar School. He had approached me one day when I was eighteen and asked me to become a Sea Cadet. I did, and thought it was great, particularly the sailing. Johnny and I became friends but it was only when we were chilling out at his house one day that I realised his agenda. We were fooling around and we ended up wrestling. I'm only a little chap and was overcome easily. With one arm twisted up my back and his legs pinning my other arm I was helpless.

"You lose, I win and claim my forfeits."

"We didn't agree any forfeits, Johnny."

"I know Kit, but you can't do anything about it so I am going to claim all your clothes as my winnings."

"What do you mean?"

"Watch me."

With that, he started to take my clothes off. He undid the buttons of my shirt and continued down, undoing my belt and the buttons of my fly.

Nothing more was said, but I did think about what Johnny had done and realised I liked it. At sailing, Johnny had a younger crew the same as I did, but I noticed he was always touching his crew. My crew noticed as well and looked at me often with a question in his eyes but never on his lips.

The next time Johnny and I were together at his house he told me.

"I am going to take your clothes off again Kit and play with your cock. This time though I am going to take it in my mouth and make you cum much better than last time. You can fight me if you like or you can let me do it and both of us can enjoy it."

I shrugged and let him do it.

"Lie on the bed Kit with your legs spread wide and your hands behind your head."

I did because there seemed little point in protesting, he could make me do anything he wanted. I watched him get undressed as well and kneel between my legs. He was very hard but despite his physical size, his cock was much smaller than mine was. With no hesitation, he took my still flaccid cock in his mouth and that felt incredible. I was completely erect in moments. Next came my balls, he had slicked his fingers and slid them over my ball sac making me gasp with the sensitivity of it. He bent my legs next, started rubbing my perineum, and just touched the entrance to my anus. The touch was amazing and jolted me. The next time his touch was firmer and I gasped but I couldn't say anything it was too sensual. He released my cock sat up and looked me in my eyes.

"Do you like that Kit?"

I whispered an affirmative reply.

"Relax, it will get better."

He slicked up three fingers and returned to sucking my cock and playing with my balls. With his other hand I felt his fingers worrying my anus and it felt fantastic. He pushed against my anus quite hard and I felt his finger penetrate me. I bucked against this invasion, but not very hard, I was experiencing a sensory overload. He pushed all the way in and hit my prostate gland. I orgasmed immediately and Johnny took my sperm in his mouth.

"Mmm, you taste sweet, Kit."

He played with me again, added another finger to the first, and started to finger fuck me. My cock was hard again almost instantly because he kept hitting my prostate. When he added the third finger I wanted to object but I was in heaven my senses were on overload, I had never experienced anything like it. Johnny pushed my legs further up and back.

"Hold your legs there Kit."

I did, not realising what he intended. He slid closer to me and I felt his cock touching my bottom. I wriggled but his head touched my rosebud and he pushed hard. I felt it pass over my sphincter and I screamed with the pain. Johnny kept still for a few minutes and when the pain decreased he fed me the remainder of his cock. It felt amazing and the sensitivity of it made me orgasm again. Johnny started to fuck me then and it was heavenly. He was very gentle and when he came, I could feel the power of his orgasm. My own senses were reeling and it was ages before I calmed down enough to understand what had happened.

"You fucked me Johnny, how could you? That was disgusting."

"Look at you Kit, you are covered in your own cum. You must have enjoyed it to orgasm that many times."

"I don't know, only queers enjoy being butt fucked, I don't want to be queer."

"Let's see what happens, Kit."

What happened was that Johnny fucked me frequently and I loved it. We sucked each other to orgasm frequently as well and I loved the sweetness of his cum.

One Monday at school when I had not seen Johnny over the weekend, he met me on one of our breaks.

“You will never guess what I did over the weekend.”

“No but I bet you are going to tell me.”

“I fucked my crewman.”

“I don't believe you Johnny, there is no way little Trevor would let you do that.”

“Yes there is, he was begging for it. I have been sucking him and finger fucking him for ages, even before you and I got it on. He was more reluctant than you were. Now it's your turn to get your crewman into it.”

“No way man, it's ok with you but I'm not involving Bobby in it.”

“We'll see. I have organised for all of us to meet at my house on Wednesday afternoon. No school that day, local elections.”

I had my first fuck then and it was amazing. Trevor turned out to be a real cock slut. When he saw the size of mine, he wanted it inside him. Bobby was open-mouthed watching it and nearly fainted when Johnny took him in his mouth. It was quite an afternoon. I don't know how many times I came but I fucked Trevor twice, sucked Bobby off in a 69er while Johnny fucked me, it was truly amazing.

I had nearly two years of this fantastic sex eventually fucking Bobby and letting him fuck me.

The sailing was terrific with me taking honours frequently. I was determined after my exams to join up but my parents wanted me to do my advanced certificates and go on to university.

We didn't have much money but my Dad told me I would be the first person in our family to go to university. I didn't want to, I wanted to be a Navy Engineer and do lots of sailing. I won in the end and joined up to go to Navy College for four years to study Marine Engineering.

I loved it from day one. For the first four weeks it was induction. Lots of marching and physical exercise and of course my beloved sailing. Although I was the same age as the others in my class I was small, only five feet seven inches, but I had a great body. My abs were incredible because of all the sitting up and back I had to do when racing my dinghies, probably several hundred sit ups every race, the rest of me developed because of my programme to keep fit. I was popular with the physical education staff because I was so keen and so fit.

The parade gunners were another story, they were bullies and I took the brunt of their bullying because I was small. That actually helped my fitness because I was always running round the parade ground with a rifle held above my head as a punishment. When they realised I didn't count that as a punishment, they found something nastier.

It happened in my fourth week.

“Not good enough again today Mr. Sherwood, report to the armoury after your final period.”

“Yes Sir.” Was all I could say. I knew that the main reason they bullied me was because I looked too young and in seven or eight years time I would be a chief, and they would still be petty officers.

The armoury wasn't a proper one. The only thing kept in it was the training rifles for us youngsters. The gunners had moved in some furniture and turned it into a sort of recreation room. They had a mess table and some chairs and sofas.

I didn't know what to expect when I knocked and entered after final lessons for the day. No one else had reported here for punishment. There were four leading gunners and two petty officer gunners there when I walked in. The senior of them walked behind me and locked the door.

“Don't want to be disturbed while we punish you boy do we?”

I had no idea what he meant so I agreed.

“Er, no Sir.”

“You are continually under performing on the parade ground Sherwood so we think you need some proper punishment.”

I knew that wasn't true but I couldn't argue.

“What punishment was meted out to you at school for poor performance?”

“We used to be caned Sir.”

“Well we are going to do the same. Strip.”

I looked aghast at the gunner.

“What Sir?”

“Strip, take your clothes off. “

“We were caned clothed Sir.”

“Well you aren't going to be here. Let me help you. First, take off your cap.”

I did.

"Now your jacket."

Shoes, tie, and shirt followed.

"Now your trousers."

"But Sir."

"Do it Sherwood or I will have you up on a charge, refusing to obey a superior officer."

So I did.

The Navy issued us with what nowadays we call boxers but in those days they were such an awful shape we used to call them passion killers so, for two reasons, I wore tight white briefs, for comfort and to hold in my substantial penis, even when soft it was very obvious in the passion killers.

With just my briefs on, the gunners could all make out that I was more than adequately hung.

"Your underpants now Sherwood, let's see your crown jewels."

I was mortified but did as I was told. As soon as I had them off, I covered my genitals with my hands.

"Attention Sherwood."

The senior gunner pulled up a chair to within about three feet of me and using his swagger stick lifted my cock up.

"What do you call this Mr. Sherwood?"

I was so embarrassed I didn't know what to say until I was asked the question again.

"It's my penis, Sir."

"Are you sure Mr. Sherwood? It looks to me like you stole it from a real man."

I blushed, and blushed even more when one of the other gunners said.

"It can't get any bigger when it's hard Tom, he just stays long when flaccid."

Tom lifted it further and kind of stroked the underside with his stick pushing it against my belly. At eighteen years old, my cock needed virtually no stimulation so very quickly I was completely erect.

"Oh Christ Tom I was wrong! That thing is a monster."

"How long is it boy?"

"I don't know Sir."

"Anyone got a tape measure? I have to measure this one."

They had and Tom gasped after he had the figures.

"This little bugger has ten and a half inches and it's seven inches round."

"Well we can soon get rid of that. Let's punish him and send him on his way."

They had me lie on the table on my tummy and four of them grabbed a limb each and stretched me wide. Tom then used his swagger stick to deliver six strokes. They hurt but I didn't cry.

"Stand up boy."

I did and they could see my distress and my resolve not to cry, my cock was back to flaccid.

"Get dressed boy and pray you are better on the parade ground tomorrow because punishment will get worse if we have to call you in again."

I was very unhappy with that statement.

* * *

The next day was great, the Gym was terrific and the Physical Training Instructors were full of praise for my performance.

"We could use you in the gymnastics team, young Sherwood."

That was from the senior instructor.

"Thank you Sir, I would like that but not if it interferes with my sailing."

"Hmm, you will have to leave that one with me. Perhaps we can work something out."

I felt so good. Academics were the same. All of our instructors were Lieutenants with degrees in things like Engineering, Maths, and the Sciences. They were full of praise for me. The only blot on my day was parade training last period.

"Not good enough, Sherwood," was the Parade Gunner's comment.

It was the first time that I knew I was being picked on. I had done as well as everyone else. Wrong thing to do I was to realise later, but I protested.

"I'm sorry Sir, but I am sure I have done as well as everyone else."

"You are now a parade expert Sherwood, are you?"

"No Sir, but I know I am no worse than anyone else."

"Well perhaps we had better discuss it after this period. Report to me in the armoury."

The two Petty Officer Gunners were the only ones there on this occasion.

"Come in Sherwood, lock the door."

"Now, whether you were as good as the rest of your class or not is immaterial. You argued with a superior officer and should be charged with insubordination. I am going to offer you a choice. You take my punishment or the Captain's."

For me there was no choice. I wanted a clean disciplinary sheet when I joined the fleet because I was ambitious.

"Your punishment, Sir."

I saw him look at the other Gunner with a smirk on his face.

"Very well boy, strip."

I knew the routine and was naked, stood at attention in front of him in double quick time.

"Stand at ease boy, --- now spread your legs wider and put your hands behind your head."

I did but was shocked with his next action. He took my cock in his hand and started to play with it. I blushed furiously, tried to step back, but was stopped by his other hand on my bottom.

"Sir, that is not right."

"You have accepted my punishment boy and that will be anything I consider right."

When I was hard, he continued stroking my penis, made his other hand slippery with spit and started to fondle my balls as well. I was beginning to lose it I was so turned on so he made me climb up on the mess table on my knees with my legs spread and my head resting on my arms.

"Push your bottom back boy."

I did but jumped forward again very quickly when he touched my bum.

"Keep still or you are going to feel some serious pain."

He resumed stroking my bottom and eventually started to run his fingers down my crack to my rose bud. A finger entered me and I started to cry.

"Please don't do that Sir. That is disgusting."

"Be quiet boy, it feels as though you have had fingers up there before."

I said nothing, I didn't want him to know I had been fucked a zillion times. His finger was doing fantastic things inside me and by the time he added the third one my pre-cum was almost a continuous stream, but I was still crying I felt so humiliated.

"Roll onto your back boy and swing your legs over your head spread wide."

I was mortified. One of the Petty Officers was finger fucking me and the other one wanked me to orgasm. I then received ten very hard slaps on my butt by the hands of the gunners.

Back in my dormitory, my mates wanted to know what happened. It was obvious I had been crying so I had to tell them I had been spanked but I didn't tell them the rest.

My best friend was Nigel and he comforted me.

“I don't think they are allowed to administer corporal punishment, Kit. You could report them.”

“No one will believe me, Nig. I'm just a first term grunt.”

“Well we have to do something. It's not fair the way they pick on you. You are an ace guy.”

* * *

The first four weeks were over, leave was granted and Nig and I had our first run ashore. It was great, he was a Duke of Edinburgh's Gold Award winner and a Rover Scout so he was full of adventurous ideas. We explored the local area and ended up on a small grassy headland overlooking a pretty bay.

Life was always fun with Nigel and active as well. The problem was that like Johnny Johnson, Nigel was much bigger and stronger than I was so when we roughhoused he always won. This afternoon was no different and after a few minutes of wrestling, I was the one unable to move. I was no pushover but I just wasn't big enough or strong enough. He had incapacitated me in such a way that the elbow of his right arm was in my groin. Moving it around a bit he had me hard as iron.

“Come on Nig, that's enough, let me go now.”

“Mmm, I don't know, this feels interesting under my arm. I wonder if I should explore further.”

“Hey, the gunners are bad enough without you joining them.”

As soon as I said it I wanted to bite my tongue.

Nig looked shocked and then curious.

“What do you mean about the gunners, tell me Kit?”

“No forget it, it's nothing.”

“I'm not forgetting it Kit. Tell me or I debag you and then do unspeakable things to your private parts.”

“Don't, Nig. I can't tell you.”

“Yes you can. I'm your best friend here, you can tell me anything.”

I decided to tell him, everything. I cried with embarrassment as I unfolded the tale of my two punishment sessions in the armoury. He was open mouthed with shock at the end of it.

“Jesus, Kit. That is so humiliating.”

Nothing else was said and we returned to the ship in time for supper.

Our new routine started on the Monday and left us with only one parade ground session a week. Our days were split into three, Academics, Workshop and Sport. Just one-day's sport session was devoted to the parade ground and weapons training.

The first session was weapons training in which I excelled. The gunners could find nothing to complain about because everything was based on competitiveness. The second part was complex parade ground drills. With such a first class brain, I handled the drills no problem but the gunners criticised me. Nigel was incensed.

"Chris Sherwood was the best on the parade ground, Sir. It's most unfair to keep picking on him."

"Oh so you're now an expert, Brown. Take yourself round the parade ground three times with your rifle over your head. Sherwood, the armoury. Class dismissed."

As soon as I was in the armoury, I had to strip. The gunners forgot the door and Nigel. When he opened the door to return his rifle, he saw me stood naked with the gunners sat all round me.

"Er, I'm returning my rifle, Sir."

"Get out, Brown."

Nig went, but not before he had given me a good once over inspection with his eyes.

"You are getting too big for your boots, Sherwood, so I think we need to up your punishment and humiliation. On all fours, spread your legs and lift your head."

The youngest gunnery instructor pulled his shirt off, dropped his trousers and pants, and now totally naked knelt before me and made me suck him.

"Use your hands as well, Sherwood, I want the best blowjob ever from you."

He was beautifully equipped and I had no problem with sucking him. One of the other gunners went behind me and started finger fucking me. He stretched me so wide it hurt and I started to cry with the pain. When the gunner in my mouth had cum I was able to voice my feelings.

"Sir that hurts so much, please don't stretch me anymore."

I received a hard slap on my butt and was told to keep quiet. Another gunner stripped and face fucked me quite violently and shot most of his sperm over my face, rubbing it in and then making me lick his hand clean. The next bit was destructive. I received twenty cuts with a swagger stick. I was screaming at the end of it.

As the punishment finished the door opened and Nigel came in with the Officer of the Day and the Master at Arms. They could see immediately what had been going on. The young gunner was still naked and the gunner who had beaten me was still stood over me with his swagger stick in hand and a very tented pair of uniform trousers showing his arousal quite clearly. My arse was a mess.

For me, the court martial of all the gunners was a source of huge embarrassment. I had to tell the court everything that went on in my three punishment sessions. It was held partly in camera so Nigel was the only one from my course who heard the details.

Prison and dishonourable discharge was the verdict on all of them and no parade training for a week for us while they drafted in some new parade staff.

Everyone was curious but Nigel and I would tell them nothing more than that the gunners had been abusing me.

The next semi traumatic happening in my life was in the place I least expected anything to happen, the Gym.

I was accepted into the Gymnastics team on the understanding that my Sailing came first.

When the time approached for our first match the Gymnastics Physical Training Instructor, (P.T.I.) pulled me out of a training session.

"Right young Sherwood, we need to fit you out for competition. Let's go down to the kit room."

Once there he told me to strip to my jock.

"I don't wear a jock strap, Sir."

"Well how do you support yourself when exercising?"

"I wear my underwear, Sir."

"Well that's not acceptable. You know you aren't supposed to wear your normal clothes for gym."

"Yes Sir, but I don't own a jock strap."

"Ok Kit, what size are you?" His voice had softened and I realised he was very young to be a P.T.I. and he was also very nice, no harsh words from him or anything like that.

"Small, Sir."

"Ok, slip out of your clothes and we'll dress you from the skin up."

I was so embarrassed getting naked in front of this very young buffed and good-looking P.T.I. but he was very diplomatic and just passed me a jockstrap from the storage bin without looking back at me.

When I had it on, he turned round and dropped down in front of me.

"I'm just going to adjust this Kit before we try your display shorts."

He pulled the straps around a bit and because his face was only a couple of feet from my crutch and he was touching my skin I started to bone up. He moved back a little and just watched my cock grow to full erection, open mouthed.

"Christ Kit, that is amazing. There is no way we are going to be able to hide that in your tight shorts. Try this pair and let's look. "

I slid the tight shorts over my jock strap and the P.T.I. sat back and laughed.

"I'm sorry Kit, I was just imagining what would be said if you performed in that state. The shorts are right but if you get a hard on in competition we are going to be in trouble. That is an amazing piece of equipment."

I was blushing but my instructor was making it so easy to join him in his merriment of my cock size. We were both giggling like kids when he next spoke.

"Kit, you are a very special guy. Will you call me Tim when we are away from authority?"

"I'd like that Tim."

"So what do we do with that thing between your legs?"

I thought about it a bit and decided to bite the bullet.

"Just before I start competing Tim, I will have to slip into a toilet and have a wank."

"That is what I was going to suggest but I didn't want to embarrass you. There is however one problem with that idea. Your first exercise you have your hands bandaged for. Can you still wank like that?"

"Oh shit, I don't know."

"Embarrassing Kit but would you like to try if I bandage you up?"

I thought he meant in private so I said no problem. He bandaged my hands and then said.

“I'll get rid of your shorts.”

He did and my jockstrap. I was stood there naked and hard.

“Oh God Kit, you are beautiful and that cock is to die for.”

I was truly flattered. Tim was a gorgeous guy. I said I would do it and started to wank.

“It's not working, Tim.”

He took over, looking me in the eyes all the time. He felt so good and it showed in the speed with which I orgasmed.

“Oh crikey Tim that was amazing.”

He leant forward and kissed me very gently on the lips.

“I want to make love to you Kit, you are so beautiful.”

I was flattered by Tim's attention but didn't think it was warranted. I was five foot seven and 140 lbs. I was dark haired with deep blue eyes, I suppose you would say I had elfin features which made me look younger than I was. The body was in good shape and the butt was tight. My package was too big for my little frame so even soft it was obvious, that was why I wore tighty whities, not that we called them that in those days, they were Y fronts.

“Thank you Tim, I would like you to.”

“We could go to prison if we were caught Kit but I would risk it to do it.”

"Nigel Brown is my best friend here, when we have our long weekend in two weeks time I can't go home, it's too far, so I am going home with him. He will understand if I want to slip away to spend time with you. You just have to find somewhere for us to make love, Tim."

Nothing more was said, I competed in Gymnastics with Tim as my mentor. He gave me several wonderful hand jobs and I went ashore with Nigel again.

That was another landmark. We ended up on the same headland as before and Nigel dominated me.

"I have seen you naked Kit but I want to see you naked and hard."

"Oh come on Nig, are you going kinky for me as well."

"Honestly Kit, yes. You don't appear to have any idea how beautiful and sexy you are. You have so much between your legs that no one can have any doubt that you are seriously rigged and I would love to fuck you until I can't get hard anymore."

Nigel was special so what could I say.

"Ok Nig, for the next half an hour you can do anything you like to me."

Nigel undressed me completely and then himself. He played with my penis, licked it a few times and then concentrated on my butt. He had me on my tummy with my legs spread and he stroked me and kissed my cheeks and the bits in between for ages before lubing fingers to start stretching me. I came up on my knees and started begging him to fuck me.

Part 2

First Naval Penetration

"Please Nig feed me your cock. I want you to breed me."

He did, easing into me gently. He was quite small which was disappointing I was definitely turned on to take a monster. His screwing motion was very thrilling though and I came several times before he did as well. While we were cuddling afterwards Nigel cried and told me how much he loved me. I was amazed.

My life was getting complicated. My best friend and my favourite P.T.I. were in love with me and wanted to get their cocks inside me.

"Nig, when we go on our long weekend, Tim wants to have some time with me. He is in love with me as well as you. I like both of you very much but I'm not in love with either of you, I just love sex. Will you be very upset if I go off with him for a little while?"

"Mum and Dad aren't going to be at home on Sunday and Monday Kit, Tim can stay over on the Sunday night if you like and you can sleep with either or both of us. Please let me have you to myself on Friday and Saturday."

"Hey Nig that's great, of course you can have me Friday and Saturday. I'm sure Tim will love to stay on Sunday and travel back with us on Monday."

Next Gymnastics training I engineered it that Tim had to go down to the store and I volunteered to help him.

"Tim, Nigel Brown says you can spend Sunday and Monday with us and sleep overnight. We may end up with threesomes. Nigel loves me and I think he will be upset if I stay with you even though he has said he won't."

"Kit as long as I can make love to you, the whole world can watch."

"Can we charge an entry fee then, Tim?"

He looked at me and we both creased up with laughter.

"You tart, I bet you would as well."

He grabbed me and planted a deep kiss on my lips.

"I love you little man."

"Don't Tim, let's go back."

* * *

Friday lunch time we all departed for the long weekend. Tim had Nigel's address and arranged to be with us Sunday morning. Train to Exeter, change to a local line for Crediton. Nig's parents were great.

"We've put a camp bed in your room, Nigel. We thought you and Chris would like to sleep in the same room."

Nig and I looked at each other and just smiled.

There were no showers in Nig's parent's house so we shared a bath at bedtime.

"I am going to wash you Kit, kneel up while I wash your cock."

He washed my entire front, being very sensual, bringing my nipples and my cock to full erection. I loved it.

"Turn round Kit and bend forward."

He then repeated the exercise. He used a well-soaped finger to penetrate me and worried my prostate for a while.

"Stop Nig or I am going to cum."

I did the same to him except that he wouldn't let me penetrate him.

"I'm not gay Kit, I just love you."

I was gob smacked.

Nigel made love to me that night with a tenderness I couldn't believe. He sucked me and rimmed me, all very gay things.

"How could you suck me and rim me Nig if you aren't gay?"

"I don't know. All I know is that I would do anything to please you and show you how much I love you."

He showed me again on Saturday night, it was marvellous.

I was eighteen and a half years old, the year was 1958, homosexuality was illegal and not discussed, But my best friend who was not gay had taken me to paradise with his lovemaking, confusing or what. If Tim made love to me and told me he wasn't gay I think it would have blown my mind.

The reality was much easier to take.

Tim arrived at lunchtime on Sunday just as Nig and I arrived back from the pub. We grabbed a snack and took it through to the lounge.

"Tim, how old are you?"

"I'm twenty one, Kit, why?"

"Because I want a more mature person than Nigel or me to explain something. Nig says he isn't gay, he just loves me. But he has made love to me in such a way that I find it difficult to believe a straight man could. If you do the same and tell me you aren't gay I'm going to be very confused."

Tim laughed before replying.

"I know a few straight men that will indulge in gay sex Kit if the other person is someone they like. When I have sex with you this weekend or ever it will be because I love you and I am gay. Nigel, please keep my secret. You know if we are discovered doing the things we have been doing to Kit we will go to prison."

"Yes, I know Tim, we learnt a little about homosexuality on my Duke of Edinburgh Course. I think I must be bi-sexual really because I sucked and rimmed Kit and I guess straight boys don't go that far. Tim, I'm not going to interfere tonight. You can have my bedroom with Kit and I will sleep in the spare room."

"Thanks Nigel I appreciate that. I've wanted to make love to this little bombshell from the first day I saw him so it will be nice not to share him tonight."

It was great to see Tim so relaxed with me, which had never happened before. We always had to be on our guard when we were on board ship, (our ship was a shore establishment or more correctly, a stone frigate.)

The afternoon and evening went very well. We played cards, listened to the radio and talked, mostly about our hopes and dreams. Tim wanted to go into sports management when his engagement was completed. Nig wanted to have his own electrical business and I wanted to be marine superintendent for an oil company. For the present, I just wanted Tim to make love to me. Well he did have a body and looks to die for.

We bathed together that night, very much a mirror action to my previous two nights with Nig. When we got into bed, Tim leant up on one elbow looking down on my body.

"You are truly beautiful Kit, and I am going to take a long time exploring your body."

"Yes please Tim, I want you to make love to me, I want to feel you inside me."

He started with my face, kissing my eyes, nose, ears, cheekbones and eventually my lips. Everything he did was done so gently it was like a whisper, it barely disturbed me, but it was so sensual I was erect in moments.

Next came the hands, like his lips, soft and gentle, over my chest, tweaking each nipple as his fingers roamed over them, at the same time nuzzling my neck with his lips. The hand slid lower gently rubbing my belly and scooting over my pubic hair, back and forth, just touching the base of my cock with his fingertips and the topside of my cock with the back of his hand.

The lips and tongue came next. The teeth were used on my nipples, making me jump and moan with the sensitivity of it. He licked out my inny belly button before running his tongue over my cock head, playing with my ball sac at the same time. Nothing in my life had prepared me for this, it felt as though Tim had electric probes on the end of each finger. I was moaning and wriggling in an ecstasy of sensations. He ran his tongue down the underside of my shaft and that was it for me, I started to orgasm, Tim missed the first jet of my sperm but took the rest in his mouth sucking me completely dry before releasing my cock.

I started to cry.

"I'm sorry Tim, I've spoilt it for you, I'm really sorry, I couldn't stop it."

He slid back up the bed and kissed me, as always, gently.

“Shhh, you have nothing to be sorry for. I am so flattered that I can turn you on so much, so quickly.”

He slid back down, licking up my cum as he went and resumed where he left off. His left hand was roaming my torso again and his mouth started to devour my balls moving up and down my shaft at intervals. When I was rock hard again he took my glans in his mouth and swirled his tongue round it making me go ballistic.

“Oh God Tim, stop I am going to cum again.”

He pulled off me and changed his position so that he was kneeling between my legs. I was gasping and wondering what he was planning next. I hadn't touched him but I could see that his cock was like a rod of iron it was so hard, it was also a very respectable length and thickness. I knew when he entered me I would be in cock heaven but he didn't appear to be in any hurry as he started to lick the inside of my thighs. Every time he reached the top of my thighs he swabbed my ball sac while his left hand continued to caress my tummy and my nipples. When I was squirming with the pleasure of it all again he pushed my legs back further and started to lick my anal entry as well. His tongue was driving me wild. I had never known sensations like it. Tim took a break from my nether regions then and came back to my face, lots more kisses and little words of endearment.

“I love you Kit, you are spectacularly sexy.”

He then started all over again licking his way down my body nipping my nipples and moving on back down to my cock which once again he swallowed. I could feel his tongue washing the shaft before he pulled off and attacked my ball sac and perineum. After almost an hour of this Tim started to open me up with his fingers and then went back to tonguing me. He pushed it as deep into my anus as he could and then sucked. I thought he was going to suck my insides out. Quite suddenly it all stopped and he pushed my legs even further back and wider before pushing an incredible cock into me right to the hilt.

"Oh crikey Tim, that feels indescribably good. I can feel every inch of you."

Starting slowly with plenty of hip movement, he had me orgasming very quickly. And as he sped up and pushed in further and harder I had multiple orgasms. I felt him swelling inside me prior to cumming and his last few strokes were so forceful I screamed with the feeling of being totally consumed by his monster. As Tim fell forward on me, I burst into tears.

"Oh Baby have I hurt you?"

"Oh no Tim, that was just the most incredible loving I have ever experienced. You really do love me, don't you?"

"Yes Baby always."

I felt so secure in Tim's arms, I didn't think anything would ever hurt me again if I had him to protect me.

A fantastically happy and satisfied young man returned to his ship the next day.

Nig realised that I loved Tim and vice versa so he never touched me sexually again, we remained best friends and he was my protector until we went off to part two training.

Tim and I spent an awful lot of time frustrated, we could get together for sex so seldom. A quick blowjob in the equipment store occasionally, but always worrying about being caught took the joy out of it.

We escaped for the odd weekend and Tim spent all my leaves with me. Our love deepened and so did our frustration. Eighteen months flew by and I headed for Scotland for part two training. Nigel headed to Portsmouth for his and Tim stayed where he was.

For the next two and a half years, I had sex only on leave, with Tim of course, apart from the rape by Barry.

In our part one establishment we were introduced to sprogging. It was a bit like public schools where the new boys have to do tasks for the seniors. Because our seniors were only about a year older than we were, sprogging was light and often fun. In our part two training college the age difference could be as much as three years so it all got a bit more serious. It all started about our second or third day. Boys from the senior class came wandering around our dormitories to pick their sprog for the term. One of the Petty Officer Apprentices picked me, they were like prefects. This one was in charge of a dormitory full of his own classmates.

“Hello, I'm Barry Latham. You are going to be my sprog for the term.”

I replied, “Hello, I'm Chris Sherwood but everyone calls me Kit.”

“Well everyone other than sprogs call me Barry, you will call me Petty Officer Apprentice Latham.”

“That's quite a mouthful, wouldn't Sir be easier and quicker.”

He looked at me hard to try to figure out if I was taking the piss. Which I was, I thought he was pompous.

“What a good idea sprog. Now, I hope you clean shoes and bull boots really well because that will be your main task for me.”

“Yes Sir, no problem.”

I was good at bulling parade boots so if that was all I had to do I wouldn't mind.

I settled in happily, or as happily as I could without Tim. Barry gave me no problem because his boots were brilliant. My dormitory P.O. Apprentice was a nice guy who mothered us. His name was Paddy Murphy. He wasn't Irish at all, but with his surname, he had picked up the nickname.

One morning I was a bit tardy getting out of bed and Paddy got me out by shock treatment.

"Sherwood, stand by your bed, now."

The 'now' was very loud and I was at attention in an instant. Problem was I slept in my passion killers because I didn't like pyjamas and I only wore my tighty whities when clothed. Passion killers didn't hide very much so my morning glory was very obvious. Paddy didn't say anything but he sure looked shocked.

The unpleasant evening that happened a few days later was because of a conversation in the senior apprentice's lounge that I pieced together sometime later.

* * *

"How are you getting on with your brood of new sprogs, Paddy?"

"No problem, Barry. They have to be the best course I have seen above or below us."

"How so?"

"Academically they are superior, with young Sherwood top of the lot. He will probably be offered a fast track to a commission. He already has the educational qualifications. He is also rumoured to be good enough to get an Olympic trial in sailing and he is a better than average gymnast. Something else about him, Barry. He has a fucking enormous cock."

"How do you know?"

“I made him jump out of bed the other morning and he was throwing a boner. It has to be a foot long.”

“Oh come on Paddy that is unbelievable. He isn't much bigger than that himself.”

“Ha, ha. Believe me it is.”

Barry obviously intended to find out and devised a little game to ensure he did. I was finishing off a letter to Tim when a messenger poked his head in the door and called out three names.

“Burton, Sherwood, Watkins. Report to Petty Officer Apprentice Latham dressed in gym kit.”

When we arrived, the total of my course in the senior dorm was eight. The other seven were probably the biggest guys in my term.

“We are going to play a game sprogs. Strength exercises. Each time you lose, you lose a life. Each life is an article of clothing or a forfeit. Two at a time play and when you lose you stay for the next game. We play a minimum of eight games and we stop after that when someone has to pay a forfeit.”

Names were drawn for the first game, Sherwood and Watkins. The first game was arm wrestling and I lost. The next game was proper wrestling to a fall and I lost. You guessed. I lost all eight games.

“Ok, the rest of you can leave. Sherwood, centre stage at attention.”

When everybody in my class had left, Barry told me to start retrieving my lives by taking my clothes off. Shoes and socks only counted one life per pair. I was down to my briefs and I stopped.

“That's only four Sherwood, keep going.”

“Sir, this isn't right.”

“Don't argue Sherwood, we can make your first term very unpleasant if you don't play the game.”

Implied threat worked. I took my briefs off and stood covering my groin.

“Attention Sherwood.”

I did and the whole bunch of seniors gasped with one comment being heard.

“Christ and that is soft.”

“Sherwood, we have three lives left for forfeits. For your first one, play with yourself until you are erect.”

“Sir, that isn't right.”

“We've heard that one before, do it or I will do it for you.”

I did but it took me ages I was so embarrassed. When I was hard Barry produced a ruler and laid it along the top of my cock.

“Huh, Paddy said it was a foot, it's only ten and a half.”

“Crikey Barry, I'd be happy with a lot less than that.”

While this was going on they had produced a litter that looked like a sacrificial table and I had to lie on it at attention. They hafted it up and walked me to the next dorm.

“We have a sacrifice to the god of phallus. We thought you might like to see him. Stay hard Sherwood or you are in trouble.”

So, blushing like hell I played with myself every time it started to flag. I was paraded through all four seniors' dorms like that. Back in Barry's dorm came the next piece of humiliation.

“We've seen the incredible front, for your second forfeit we are going to see the back. Stand up close to the mess table one foot away from it, legs astride and bend over until your chest is resting on it. -------- Now spread your legs wider and use your hands to pull your arse cheeks as wide as you can.

“Please Sir that is disgusting.”

“Do it Sherwood, you are beginning to piss me off.”

I did it blushing deep scarlet all over my body I thought.

Barry started stroking my back then getting lower all the time until he was stroking my arse.

“Put your hands back on the table.”

I did and felt him pulling my cheeks apart sliding his thumbs in to touch my anus.

“No, you mustn't do that Sir.”

One of the other seniors agreed.

“Barry, you are going over the top, you could be in trouble if you continue.”

No penetration but I did get a couple of hard slaps.

“Ok Sherwood on your back on the table, legs in the air and spread as wide as you can. Everyone have a good look at the rosebud, cock and balls of our little sacrifice and we'll let him go.”

I hadn't felt this humiliated since the gunners. I cried myself to sleep that night with everybody knowing that something horrible had happened to me but not daring to ask what.

A few days later I was summoned to the Chief Apprentices Cabin for twelve class. I thought that was weird because all the chief apps were away on a leadership course. Barry was there when I knocked on the door and was invited in.

"You still owe me one forfeit Sherwood and I am going to take it now. Take all your clothes off and then mine."

I didn't like him but he did have a very sexy body and a more than adequate cock, it was of course erect.

"Now I want you to suck me to orgasm swallowing all my jism."

I was pissed off at this further humiliation, but in all honesty I loved sucking on a pretty cock. Barry realised I was a practised exponent of the cocksucking art and decided to go to the next level.

"That was an amazing blowjob Kit. Now I am going to fuck you."

Boy was he good. I don't know whether it was because of me or he had plenty of experience but I orgasmed several times while he fucked me doggy fashion to start with and culminated in the missionary position.

Great sex but I loved Tim and didn't want other guys having what was rightfully his.

I decided that was the last time I would allow anyone to humiliate me because of my size and the size of my cock. The next time I had Barry's parade boots to bull I made sure the layers of polish were so thick that the second he flexed his foot in them the polish would crack and hopefully chunks would fall off. They looked incredible when I took them up to him. You could literally see your face in them. My idea worked spectacularly, they just fell apart at the toes before he got to the parade ground. Result, he was in deep shit with the gunners. I got some stick but he didn't realise I had done it deliberately, so I let him know.

“I'm sorry about your boots Sir. I guess I was distracted because of my thoughts on your abuse of me. I don't suppose it will happen again unless I am abused by a sexually deviant sadist in the senior class.”

He had the good grace to blush but Paddy told me that the word had gone out to all seniors that I was not to be touched again. I of course never told Tim.

One year in the Mediterranean as a third engineer, nearly two years in the Far East climbing to first engineer and then back to England to be an instructor in Portsmouth almost the youngest chief in the Royal Navy.

I wrote to Tim every day for my year in the Med. When I returned to the U.K. he was overseas with a gymnastics display team. Letter frequency then dropped, once a week, once a month, and then nothing. I still had no sex with anyone else. I cried for my lost love often but I knew it was a hopeless situation. The chances of being in the same country together were remote, to get leave together almost no chance at all.

I applied for a commission and my papers disappeared into the system for my assessment so despite the fact that I was a Chief I remained in Petty Officers Rig waiting to be officially rated.

I moved into the mess in barracks and was allocated a large two-birth cabin. It was a conversion in the upgrade of the Petty Officers Mess so I even had an en suite bathroom.

“Your cabin mate is away with the united services ski team so you should have this cabin to yourself for a while,” I was informed by my orderly.

I did and got used to it. When I came back in from work one day and saw the bags by the other bunk I knew my peace was over. I was working away at my desk when the door opened and a voice started to say,

“Hi, I'm Tim --“

As he started to speak, I swung round in my chair and stood up. Our eyes met and I collapsed in a dead faint. I came to sometime later wrapped in Tim's arms.

I cried as I looked into those wonderful grey eyes that I hadn't seen for three years.

“Oh God, please tell me you are real.”

“I'm real Baby, are you?”

“Yes Tim I'm real. I love you, I've missed you so much. I gave up believing we would ever be together again.”

Apart from work, you would have thought we were joined at the hip. We both had three years of sexual frustration to get rid of. If I am honest, we didn't make love for the first month so much as rut like animals. As soon as we got the door locked in our cabin, we just tore our clothes off and fucked. When we couldn't get hard any more we went to eat. It was wonderful and crazy.

I went for my officer selection and was offered a five-year short service commission. Of course, I accepted and prepared to head for Dartmouth Royal Naval College for my officer training.

“You need to get fit Kit. Why don't you join me in the gym for some circuit training?”

“Yuk, I haven't been near a gym since I left training. Hell will freeze over before you get me in one again.”

I guess three years at sea had killed my fitness regimen to the point where I didn't want to know. Fortunately at my age my body shape had not suffered.

"How long have we got then Kit before you go?"

"Just over a month Tim, then I have a month's leave before changing roles."

"I have a month as well before I have to return to the slopes, and then I am due a posting as well, hopefully in the U.K. so that we can still see each other."

"Oh God Tim I don't think I could stand another long spell without you. I am going to do my five years and then come out and I will follow you round the world if I have to."

Our lovemaking became desperate again. I went on leave, Tim went back to the slopes.

* * *

Dartmouth looked awesome when all my entry arrived at Kingswear Station. We carried out our induction over the next few days finishing at the gym. We lined up waiting on our new instructor. When he came in I nearly died. He saw me at the same time as I saw him and our grins were a mile wide.

"Good Morning Gentlemen, welcome to hell. I am P.T.I. Lynton, you will be expected to address me as Petty Officer Lynton or P.T.I. Lynton. Unfortunately, it is going to get very cold here because Cadet Sherwood told me hell would freeze over before I got him into a gym again."

It was no good, neither of us could keep it together I was rolling on the floor holding my sides and Tim was holding on to the wall bars. My classmates must have thought we were mad.

"Come on Kit, what's with you and our P.T.I.?"

We were in the main dormitory after work had finished for the day.

"Ok, ok. Tim Lynton was my Gymnastics Instructor when I was eighteen and we became firm friends. We met up again when I was an engineering instructor at Pompey before coming here. He is my closest and dearest friend. End of story."

"Kit, being serious, how will you two handle you being in the Wardroom and him being in the Petty Officers Mess?"

"With difficulty I expect. But I'm not going to be in the Navy forever and nor is Tim."

What a fabulous nine months I had. Sailing every day, six hours of sex most Saturday's an occasional romp in the gym store and knowing Tim was near me. Our leave schedule was the same allowing us uninhibited contact.

Neither of us wanted to think about what would happen when Dartmouth ended. But end it did. I was twenty-six, had been in love since I was eighteen and had only spent about two and a half years with my lover. When my leave ended I had to go to Yorkshire for flying training and Tim went back to the College, I was inconsolable.

There followed four more months of no Tim before I commenced Helicopter Training at Helston in Cornwall. We managed a couple of weekends a month taking a hotel room midway between Dartmouth and Helston. I was getting desperate though. This was no good for my psyche, I wanted Tim with me every day and I started coming apart. My standards fell and I looked likely to be dropped from training. I cried most of the next weekend with Tim.

"I can't handle it anymore Tim. I'm going to let it go. If I fail flying training I can be a civilian in a couple of months then anywhere you get posted I will move to and get a job. Any job as long as I can be with you. Every day I can't be with you is wasted."

"No Kit, I know you love flying, hang in there we will work it out."

Three more weeks without Tim and I was on chop checks, a change of instructor hadn't helped, I was going downhill fast.

Another rotten trip and I was lying on my bed crying like a baby. My life was unravelling. The telephone rang and I was tempted not to answer it, but I did when it wouldn't stop ringing.

"Sub-Lieutenant Sherwood."

"Petty Officer Lynton, I wondered if you would like to join me for a drink at the pub at Mullion."

"Oh God Tim, are you serious?"

"Yes, I'm staying at the pub for a couple of days before I report to the gym at Culdrose."

"I don't believe it. I'll be there in no time."

My MG nearly flew. Tim met me in the car park.

"My room first I think."

I didn't even want sex I just wanted to hold him.

"How have you done it, you must be due another year at least at Dartmouth."

That one sentence had cost me about a gallon of tears. I loved Tim so much I was becoming a total basket case being away from him.

"You lot need a Gymnastics instructor, I volunteered. It's only a six months posting but that should suit us."

"I'll apply to live off base tomorrow then we can be together every night. Oh God Tim I was dying without you."

The boss Okayed my request, I guess he thought I would be out in a few weeks anyway. I wasn't out, I was off chop checks within a month. I passed my Instrument Rating first attempt and went onto Advanced Flying Training. Every night that neither of us were duty I was curled up in Tim's arms and every morning that we weren't duty I woke up looking into the most beautiful grey eyes ever created. I didn't want to think beyond tomorrow, I was doing great living for today.

Portland came next, Operational Flying Training. Tim most weekends even though it was a long flog for both of us. Before I knew, it was time to join my squadron, embarked on H.M.S. Hermes, East of Suez.

"I can't Tim, another whole year without you. I'll die, I can't leave you again, not for a year. I'm going to get myself Court Martialled and thrown out. I can't go Tim, I love you so much."

Tim took hold of me and shook me before looking at me hard and saying,

"Now you listen to me Sub Lieutenant Sherwood. You are a frontline operational pilot. You have worked your butt off for nearly two years to get this. You are going. Kit I love you more than my life but I am not going to let you throw this away. Go out there and make me proud of you. When you come back you will have a little over a year and a half to do, I will too and then we can be together forever. Don't let me down."

I went, I got my butt shot off in Aden but made it back to base with a few holes in my tail. I also got decorated for bravery. I knew I would get any posting I wanted when I got back. Accelerated promotion to Lieutenant and I was set. Search and Rescue based at Portsmouth. Tim was still at Dartmouth waiting a new posting. We struggled to see each other but we managed a reasonable frequency. I lived for the day I could leave.

I had been in the new job for about a month when the phone rang in my office one day when I was off duty pilot.

“Lieutenant Sherwood.”

“Good afternoon Sir, this is the Chief P.T.I. I am wondering if you would help us.”

“I will if I can Chief, but what can I do for you?”

“I understand you were a better than average gymnast once upon a time.”

I laughed, “Yes Chief you got that right. Fairy tales always start, once upon a time. But how do you know that piece of information?”

“The P.T.I. Branch is quite small Sir, sporting stars that pass through our hands get known. Sir, we don't want you vaulting or demonstrating your prowess on the parallel bars but we do need an officer for our Gymnastic Team. We have a Gymnastics Instructor but we know an officer has to head all these teams. You pull more weight than a Petty Officer Sir.”

“Yes, of course Chief, what do you need me to do?”

“Our new Instructor arrived yesterday Sir, he wondered if you could meet him to discuss the team's needs.”

“Sure, Where and when, Chief?”

“You're off duty today so on your way back to the Wardroom perhaps you could drop in at the gym for a chat with him.”

“No problem, Chief. Tell him 1630.”

“Thank you Sir, he'll be in my office.”

I didn't give it a thought and had no clue until I walked in to the Gym office at 1630 and showed that I was still a little boy. Tim was there and I cried.

“Please tell me this is what I think it is.”

He took me in his arms and let me sob out my happiness. Twenty-seven years old and a big crybaby. Tim was thirty-two and my rock. If it were possible, I loved him more each time we met. Now we would be together forever.

For eighteen months, I worked as hard as I had ever worked. I ran my flight, the Gymnastics Team and studied for my civil Aviation Licences. But the biggest consumer of my time was Tim, every night, almost every weekend, every leave. I was in heaven. I knew when this period of our lives ended we could be together forever. Our love for each other had continued to grow. He was my life. I couldn't even begin to imagine life without him. He was an awesome presence and an incredible lover.

I resigned my commission six months before the due date as required and applied for an Instructor course. Tim resigned to finish the same day as me.

I started as an assistant instructor at Shoreham and Tim used his savings to start a Fitness and Gymnastics Centre in Brighton. Neither of us had spent very much money since we met. Because of our love for each other we had avoided expensive runs ashore at home and abroad. Both of us had saved and invested sensibly, my only extravagance was my little MG, which I maintained myself. So, with my savings and the biggest mortgage we could afford we bought a four-story regency terraced house in Brighton that was nearly derelict.

Converting the house and redecorating it took us nearly four years but at the end of that time Tim had a successful Gym and I was deputy chief instructor, dual qualified fixed and rotary wing. (Aeroplanes and helicopters).

Hell didn't freeze over at Dartmouth and it didn't at Brighton when I started working out and helping out with gymnastics when I wasn't flying.

I'm not sure how long it was before we stopped making love every day but it was sure as hell a long time. We had so much to make up for. The absolute culmination of our love was the day we completed the house conversion. Tim invited all his colleagues and friends from the gym and I did the same from the flying school. Most knew we were gay and nobody worried about it because we were both popular with our associates. Try being totally in love and not being nice to people, pretty difficult. Neither of us was limp wristed queens so heteros weren't uncomfortable around us. Neither of us had time to drink very much so by the time we went to bed we were both still very sober.

“Kit, do you realise I have been in love with you now for seventeen years?”

“Mmm, nowhere near long enough. Do you realise that every one of those seventeen years I have loved you more each year?”

“Huh, you're only saying that to make me feel too guilty to leave you.”

I shot up in bed and looked into Tim's eyes. Tears were pricking the back of my eyelids.

“Oh God Tim, tell me you aren't thinking of it.”

Tim looked at me, the consternation spread across my face made him realise how devastated even a hint of separation would destroy me.

“Definitely not Baby, not now, not ever. I have never had a lover other than you and I swear I have never thought about having another one. I am going to make love to you tonight, and if you have any doubts at the end of it about my love for you I will have failed. Kit you are the most beautiful, gentle, talented, exciting, awesome lover any man could wish for. My life since the day I first set eyes on you has been filled with sun light. I have never doubted for one moment that I will love you for the remainder of my life.”

The sun was shining through our bedroom window by the time Tim had finished making love to me. I was crying with the happiness that this soul mate had pumped into me during the last few hours.

Our fairy tale didn't start, 'Once upon a time', but it did end 'Happily ever after.'

The End

Here is a sample from another story you may enjoy:

CHRIS JOHNS

BORDER Patrol

HOT GAY EROTICA

Patrolling this sector of the border was fine during the spring and summer months. Even in the autumn it was still pleasant, but now, in the winter, it was miserable. The choice appeared to be snow or rain, and always cold.

The patrols were on foot because the forest was too dense for vehicles and of course they were too noisy. The actual border had a fence and a road alongside it, but the commander thought roving foot patrols about a kilometre inside the border would catch more illegals because they would be less careful, now that they were across into Germany. Unfortunately he was proved correct. The patrols along the border road were always finding holes in the fence, but seldom caught anyone. But Heinrich and Jorge had captured hundreds in the year they had been doing it. On one wall in the small compound where they took the captured illegals they had rows of little men, indicating the number they had been able to return to Poland. They had started it as a joke.

"Just like our Luftwaffe Pilots marked their kills on the sides of their aircraft during the war," Jorge had said when they started it.

There was another separate tally in a notebook Jorge kept in his locker. That was the number they had not declared, always the young pretty ones or the just plain sexy. The two young guards were gay and would on occasions, when they captured a particularly attractive guy, offer him his freedom in return for sexual favors. It was fun and in the winter lightened up an otherwise dull down time. They were never refused. The young ones particularly would have sold their soul to be allowed into the West so there was never any forced sexual contact; the detainees were offered a simple choice. After they had been stripped and scoped out thoroughly the offer would be made.

"If you look as sexy when your penis is erect as you do now with it flaccid we will let you go, but not until after we have checked how good you can blow us and take our cocks up your arse."

Some were quite enthusiastic, others were very resentful but most just accepted it as the price for their freedom.

Petrov was one of the resentful ones, but he had such a superb slim body that Jorge wanted to keep him for days.

“He will get used to it, and then he will enjoy my cock up his arse. If he becomes very good I might keep him in my apartment in Hamburg as a permanent sex toy for use during my time off.”

Heinrich had laughed. He and Jorge had been friends since joining the army at eighteen, and had stayed together during their military service, joining the border patrol unit when they had served their enlisted time. The pay was good, the time off was brilliant so despite the rotten hours when they were on duty and the miserable weather in the winter they had stayed. Jorge was the joker and Heinrich loved him like a brother.

The capture of Petrov had been standard. The snow made it so easy to follow the illegals. They stopped covering their tracks about 100 metres inside the border. With their snowshoes on, Heinrich and Jorge could move much faster than the prey over the loose snow so even if they were seen early it didn’t matter, the chase just lasted a little longer.

A pistol held to his temple while Jorge cuffed him and fixed a lead to the cuffs soon had him resigned to his fate and he followed without any more trouble. Once inside the accommodation he was released from his restraints and told to strip. No trouble, there seldom was, once caught they knew there was no point in fighting it. They would of course serve time in a prison at home, but then they would try again.

Jorge had a good digital camera, the same as the official one. When Petrov was naked, he took only ones for his private collection. The encrypted files on his computer were a gallery of gorgeous naked Polish boys, many of them with erections. They showed gorgeous cocks and cute butts that Jorge knew he was going to slide his cock into.

When Petrov was naked, Heinrich carried out a body search, making it as humiliating as possible to subdue any thoughts of objection at a later stage.

"Spread your legs and bend over the desk, I am going to check that you are not secreting drugs on your person."

As he was talking, Heinrich was plastering one hand with a lubricant while Jorge had his revolver out ready to use. The humiliation was easy, a slow increase in the number of fingers being used to finger fuck him.

"This one has a really cute butt Jorge, your cock will think it has gone to heaven if you slide in here."

Jorge laughed and got the camera ready when he realized Petrov was not going to fight.

Using his own camera he took full length front and back. What he was faced with was a tall early 20's Polish man. He was slim built with fine muscle definition, slim waist and a gorgeous arse. Jorge could hardly contain himself, he so wanted to cup those two perfect little cheeks in his hands and then spread them so that he could see his little rosebud. Short, black hair, almost black eyes and long, but well proportioned face made for a very sexy picture.

Petrov

"You are a very sexy looking man Petrov. If you get an erection and we still like what we see, you will be invited to suck our cocks. Then we will see how good it feels to slide them into your arse. When we have enjoyed your body fully, we will let you go provided you never mention that you were captured if you are ever caught by the authorities."

The boy was obviously thinking about this, was it worth being buggered to get into Germany, and if he allowed it, would they keep their word? The risks he had already taken to get this far made him shudder, and he really didn't want to go to a prison in his motherland, they were quite grim.

Acquiesce and put it behind him when it was finished. He took his hands away from his groin and started to play with himself. When he was erect he dropped his hands to his sides and looked at his captors.

"Oh my God, Heinrich, I don't know about him sucking me, I know I am going down on him as soon as we have showered."

Petrov was surprised and pleased that whatever they were going to do to him, and make him do to them it was going to be with clean bodies. He was badly in need of this shower; he had been running and hiding for days as he approached the border. It would be heaven to be clean again.

Heinrich remained clothed and ready for action as he watched Jorge thoroughly pamper Petrov in the showers.

"This will warm you up Petrov. I can see you are still cold from your exposure. My name is Jorge and I am going to take my time to make love to you. I think you are a very sexy man."

Petrov was confused, he was expecting to be raped and humiliated, not pampered and made love to.

"How old are you?"

Petrov told him. "I am 21, Jorge." He said the name hesitantly which made Jorge laugh.

"I am 21 as well, we should be friends."

Petrov relaxed, and as he did so he took in more of this young German who was now being so nice to him. Jorge was bigger than Petrov in build, he also had a big penis which Petrov could see clearly now, and it was bigger than his. The thought of being fucked by it was not the most thrilling, but perhaps it wouldn't hurt too much if Jorge was gentle with him.

"Have you ever played with boys sexually, Petrov?"

The Pole shook his head.

"Well, I am going to have lots of fun teaching you how to pleasure me and I will do that by pleasuring you."

Jorge was thoroughly enjoying this. Petrov looked quite fierce but he was proving to be a little darling. He was gently spoken and appeared to have accepted his lot. His German was very good as well. Jorge thought he would probably meld in quite well with the German people. He was of course black haired so not a true Aryan, but lots of Germans were as well with all the interbreeding that had gone on since the war.

Jorge thoroughly soaped Petrov's body before gently fondling his cock and balls. It felt so good. The cock was very hard but the ball sac still had enough play in it to please Jorge. The Pole was clearly excited by all this attention and made no objection when Jorge told him to turn round. The butt was exquisite and Jorge couldn't resist moving in close so that his cock was lodged in the crack between the perfect little cheeks.

"You feel so good, and look so exciting. I know I am going to take you to Paradise."

The feel of another man's cock sliding up and down between his cheeks should have upset him, but Petrov realized he was enjoying it. Jorge continued to play with him and stroke him until he thought he would orgasm if it went on.

"I am almost ready to cum Jorge, you excite me so much."

Jorge was so pleased. He turned Petrov back round, made sure that both of them were free of soap and then dropped to his knees and took Petrov's cock into his mouth. Just a few inches so that he could swab the glans with his tongue. Too much for Petrov after all the stimulation, he came almost immediately and was horrified that Jorge had no time to pull off. The horror turned to surprise when he realized that Jorge was sucking him gently, taking all his cum as he went soft.

"Mmm, that tasted so good, I think I am going to want to do that again before we release you."

He stood up then, took Petrov in his arms and kissed him softly on the lips. This was amazing, Petrov didn't know what to do or say. He loved everything this German guard was doing to him.

Jorge

Heinrich was watching all of this and was as amazed as Petrov at his friend's actions. They had been together for years, and in this job for over a year and he had never seen Jorge show such affection for a detainee. Usually it was a suck and fuck before throwing them out, but here he was pampering this one in the shower and going down on him, and then kissing him. What on earth was going on?

When Jorge took Petrov through to the sleeping quarters instead of just fucking him over the desk, Heinrich knew it was time to step in.

"Jorge, this boy is just a fuck, he isn't your new boyfriend."

Jorge blushed a deep red as he looked at his friend.

"I'm sorry Heinrich. I have feelings for this man that I have never had for any of the other detainees. I want to make love to him, not just rape him. I know I have to let you have a go as well, but please, be gentle with him when it is your turn."

If you enjoyed this sample then look for **Border Patrol**.

Also by this Author:

Brotherly Love

Underworld

Revenge of the Jocks

Indian Abduction

Pleasurable Abduction

Lost

A Grip in Deep

Bullet Holes

Gay Porn Star

Delightfully Yours

Embracing the Greener Side

Promotional Desire

Aviator's Hidden Turbulence

Almost Paradise

The Hardcore Remedy

Relish Pretender

Doctor Boner

Captivated Attractions

Academically Horny

Flight of the Hornies

Empire's Desire

Erotic Physical Examination

Mauled by My Mate

Stage of Desire

Gray Pride

Billionaire Gay Lover

Picture Perfect

Greek Romance

Lights, Camera, ACTION!

My Best Bud, My Master

Hardcore Commando

I Sacrifice My Virginity for Love

Officer Hostile

The School Punisher

Undercover Pain

Antigua Romance

Guarded Emotion

Professor Voyeur

Probation Plebe

Underground Soldiers

The Body Search

Poker Slave

Boy Island

Take Me : Temptations on the Field

Isle of Temptation

Tied Down Order Taker

Blackmail Endowment

Slave to the Billionaire

The Rich Boy's Affair

More Than A Friend

Take It Off

Prisoner Of His Heart

Pacific Beach

Taboo Education

A Trade for a Trade

Check Mate

Queer

Gabriel's Hope Plantation

Chris Johns' Gay Compilation, Vol. 1

(All Is Fair In Love and War)

Chris Johns' Gay Compilation, Vol. 2

(Never Enough)

Chris Johns' Gay Compilation, Vol. 3

(Rough and Raw)

***

I REALLY LOVE Reviews!

If you enjoyed this book, please share the love and don't forget to leave a review on Amazon or the site of any other retailer you purchased this book from!

I highly appreciate your reviews, and it only takes a minute to write & post one. I can't tell you how much this means to me!

You'll find the list of all my books on my Author Central page... just in case you'd like to leave a review for other books of mine you've read but didn't have time to leave a review.

*Amazon Author Central – http://amzn.to/185Sar5

One Last Thing, For Kindle Readers...

When you turn the page, Kindle will give you the opportunity to rate this book and share your thoughts on Facebook and Twitter. If you enjoyed my writings, would you please take a few seconds to let your friends know about it? Because... when they enjoy they will be grateful to you and so will I.

Thank You!

Chris Johns
chris_johns@awesomeauthors.org

About the Author

The author has drawn from his lifetime experiences as a Marine Engineer and Helicopter Pilot to take his readers round the world with his erotic stories.

Born in a small town in middle England he joined the Royal Navy straight from school and spent four years at engineering college before going to sea. After promotion to first engineer he took a career turn and trained as a helicopter pilot. The move afforded him huge opportunity to travel both as a Naval Pilot and later as a Commercial Helicopter Pilot. His Bio Pic was taken when he was relaxing in his company's social club, serving his fellow pilots and engineers with some excellent English Ale.

Retired now in the Caribbean he took up writing to compliment his other great love, sailing.

You may also like the books by these authors:

DICK PARKER

COLIN AND DAVID

HOT GAY ROMANCE EROTICA

I was two weeks away from my twenty-third birthday and I lived with my parents and had no job. I was one of hundreds of thousands of "millennials" who had graduated from college and been unable to find a job in their field of study. Right now I'd take anything so I could get out of my parents' home and live on my own.

It's not that my parents aren't great. They are. But it's kind of sad living in the room I lived in when I was a teenager. It's not that I wasn't trying. I applied at every place that I could.

I did have a pretty good car thanks to Aunt Mary. She was my mother's only sister and she and I have been very close for years. Her husband died when I was a freshman in college and he left her well off. She lives on Lake Wisconsin on a huge place with nearly two acres of lakefront land. Her house could take care of a huge family but it was always just Aunt Mary, and her golden retriever, John. Yes, John, don't ask me how she came up with that name. I asked her once and she said he looked like a John.

Her lawn and garden were like something out of House and Garden magazine. When her husband died she put all of her energy into her home and garden. She asked me if I'd like to work for her to earn money during college and I jumped at the idea. I loved working outdoors and this was a great place to be. If I got too hot I could run out to the dock, jump into the lake, and take a swim. Aunt Mary paid me well and took care of me with great food and lots of extras.

She only had one daughter who ran off when she was seventeen and was never heard from again, so I was her favorite.

I heard mom drive up and walk to the kitchen. She came in from the garage and her eyes were all red.

"Mom? What's wrong?

"David, Aunt Mary died this morning."

My heart dropped. I stood there unable to speak.

Mom came to me and hugged me and we both wept. I couldn't believe it. Aunt Mary was as lively and vivacious as anyone I'd ever known. I thought she'd live to be a hundred.

"How, mom?"

"It was a heart attack. She was at the nursery buying plants. I suppose they were something you were going to plant soon."

"We were starting a new rose garden," I said, my voice breaking.

"They said it was very quick. She just slumped over and she was gone."

I turned and walked to my room. I lay face down on my bed and cried until I fell asleep.

I woke an hour later and got up. Mom was in the kitchen.

"Mom, what about John?"

"He wasn't with her. He's probably at her house."

"I better go and take care of him. I have a key."

"Will you bring him here?"

"I don't know. He's getting old. Maybe I'll just say there with him. I don't want to upset his life if I don't have to. I'll call you from Aunt Mary's."

I drove to the lake and followed the county road that ran past her house. I hadn't been there for a couple of weeks because the planting season was just starting so we had planned on working on the coming weekend. Now she was gone and I'd never get to garden with her again. I felt my eyes fill with tears as I drove along.

I pulled into her driveway and shut off my car. I could hear John barking in the house. I opened the front door and the big lug bounded out and began jumping all over me. He was happy to see me.

"Go make a pee," I said.

John ran off across the lawn toward the water. I watched him and then I noticed a kid on the dock next door. He was sitting on the end of their dock. He was wearing a pair of cutoff jeans and nothing else. He had a fishing pole lying next to him and there was a bobber floating on the water.

He turned and looked when I walked down by the water and called John.

"Hello," I said.

"Aye," he responded.

If you enjoyed this sample then look for **Colin and David**.

GAY EROTIC ROMANCE

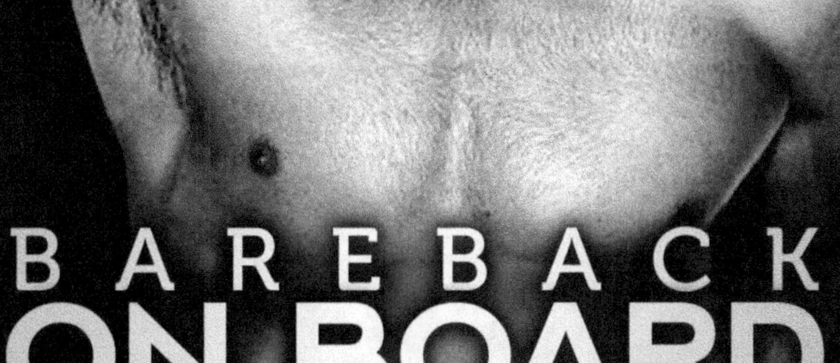

DEXTER CHASE

Twenty-four hours to go and the ship would be docking in Plymouth. The atmosphere on board was electric. Two thirds of the crew had been away for thirteen months so they were champing at the bit to get back to their loved ones. It should have only been eight months but thanks to Muslim fanatics they had remained in the Gulf to support the legitimate government as allies.

Peter de Salis was one of the other third. He had been on board for a few months learning his way around his department. He would remain in the ship for the long refit and work up with the new crew before the ship returned to South East Asia and he would move on to a new appointment.

Peter was a communications officer and stood a lot of mickey taking. Com officers had hyphenated names, or at least that appeared to be the case so he was always being told he was in the wrong branch. He was a lieutenant, head of his department at only 24 years old. He had been commissioned straight from school and therefore received his university education on the pay of a sub-lieutenant. He graduated at 21 with a first class degree, had been promoted to lieutenant straightaway, and became a communicator.

The captain believed that all of his officers should be able to run the ship if needs be, so at sea while making passage, officers like Peter would have to do a stint as second officer of the watch. A waste of time during the night watches, and that was why Peter, at two in the morning had been allowed to go down to his office to collect some paperwork he needed to do before the ship docked. He opened the door to the operations room and was about to turn on the lights when he saw a beam of light coming from the bottom of the door leading into his office. He brought out his cell phone, prepared to take some quick pictures if there was mischief afoot. No one should be in his office without his permission, and certainly not at two in the morning.

Peter opened the door and immediately took about a dozen pictures as he moved into the office and walked round the four young men that were there. They didn't move. They just looked at Peter with shocked expressions on their faces. Not surprising really. All four were naked. Two of them had their cocks up the arses of the other two.

"Watkins', I think you can remove your cocks from the Arnolds."

They did. Peter went round his desk and sat down.

"Do any of you know what punishment will be handed out at your Court Martials when these pictures are displayed?"

All four of them nodded their heads and looked terrified.

"I believe it is four years in a military prison followed by a dishonorable discharge. Let me see, you four are eighteen and nineteen so at 22 and 23 you will become civilians again after four years in prison. I imagine that will be a recipe to confirm the ruination of your lives. Would you agree with me?"

They nodded their heads more.

Adam Arnold was the baby of the four with regards to maturity and it showed. Tears were running down his cheeks. Four years seemed like an eternity to him.

Peter looked along the line of the four. These were the four communications ratings that had joined the ship with him on the same terms: remain with the ship during refit, go to sea for the shakedown with the new crew, and then be off for a new appointment. Under normal circumstance they could all have been leading ratings by the time of their new appointments. He saw Adam's tears and wanted to wipe them away then hug the boy and tell him everything would be alright.

"Charlie, how could you be so careless? Why didn't you lock the door?"

Charlie looked sick, "Didn't think anyone would be around at this time of night, Sir."

Peter shook his head. “Well, you are bloody fools, all four of you. Stand at ease.”

The four had been standing rigidly at attention until this point. Peter had scoped them out while he spoke to them and realized they were probably the most stunning young men on the ship. He was as hard as he had ever been looking at them. Fortunately, he was wearing his uniform jacket which would hide the bulge in his groin if he stood up.

If you enjoyed this sample then look for **Bareback On Board**.

A MAN'S TOY

HOT GAY EROTICA

AMY REDEK

I've still got the toy I was given when I was born and in growing up found that other boys had the same toy that I had, and in the process of getting older, still played with our toys.

I never knew my father because he was in the army and was killed somewhere in Northern India while serving his country. I was born a month after he had left and so it was only my mother that looked after me until I was able to look after myself. Which was quite early considering that mom, when I was old enough, around four years old, was to be looked after in a small crèche while she went to work in a munitions factory at the outbreak of what was known as "The Second World War".

I was taken there in the morning before she went to work and collected me in the early evening to take me home to feed, bathe and put me to bed, only having a Sunday to spend the whole day with me. I cannot say that I remember much of this, only one thing stands out clear was having to spend one night in a bomb shelter and was told later that I had cried so much that we never went into one again. We were lucky to be on the outskirt of London and so didn't have to suffer the bombing that the capital suffered.

It was a good thing that when I was five, I only had to be taken to school on that first day and from there on, went on my own and returned home well before mom came in from work.

As I grew older, I began to learn how to cook a meal so that she didn't have to worry about me being home alone and I think she appreciated having her dinner cooked for her. She had been heartbroken when she was informed that her husband had died in battle but still had me to remember him by and didn't marry again until I was sixteen.

I didn't like her choice and so stayed out of the house as much as possible, for I could never call him dad or father. I had left school at fifteen and found work as an errand boy and with this arrival of another man in the house, found a job for the evenings. This was in a hotel in the city and would start at mid-day until eight in the evening, travelling backwards and forwards by the underground train. I liked Saturdays, for they usually had functions there and so would do the extra hours until it finished and would then sleep in the cloakroom and work the Sunday morning until the afternoon, where I would then go to a cinema to watch whatever film was being shown before going home.

It was during this time that I learned that even though the country would be stopping conscription into the army sometime in the future, I would still be liable to being called up when I was eighteen. Now I could volunteer to join either the army or navy before the time arrived of my eighteenth birthday or enter the Merchant Navy, though that would mean being in there for seven years as opposed to only two in the army. The Royal Navy was seven years too, but more restrictive than the Merchant Navy, so that was what I planned to join.

I got the necessary papers finally and it took some time to get my mom to sign them, even though she knew that by me going to sea I would soon be leaving home, but also didn't want me to join the army and maybe having to go out and fight like my father had, so she signed them.

Now with the man she had married and herself, she always left home around seven thirty in the morning while I stayed in bed until they had gone before getting up. Seeing to my own breakfast, as not having to be at the hotel until mid-day, I would always see what the postman dropped through our letterbox. The day finally came when there was one brown envelope from the government that I knew would contain the order for me to do my National Service. This was three months before I would be eighteen, and so I wrote on the envelope that the person this letter was for, no longer lived at this address and posted it back on my way to take the signed paperwork to the office where they would see me to joining the Merchant Navy.

As I was still only seventeen, I would have to attend a navy school, which was at Gravesend, and they would let me know by letter the date to attend there. It was to take a course of six weeks and on passing, would be allocated to a ship. It was a month before this letter arrived giving me the date to attend this school, which was another four weeks later. This meant that I would then be eighteen by the time I finished at the school and would therefore not be classed as a boy rating. Oh, it was the catering department that I had applied for as opposed to being a deck hand for if I would be at sea in a winter time, it would be warmer being on the inside of the ship than out on deck.

In the meantime, another letter had come from the government asking mom where I might be contacted for my joining the army. She showed me this and didn't quite know what to say in reply. I told her to just say that I had since joined the Merchant Navy. So that cleared that problem.

I'd already given in my notice to the hotel that I would soon be leaving to join the navy and had a little party given me on my last day working there as I would on the following Monday have to report to the Gravesend school. Mom was in tears on that day when I left at six a.m., consoling her by saying that I would be back in six weeks time before having to finally go to sea.

I duly turned up at the school on time, following others with their suitcases and saw that it looked like a prison that we would be spending the next six weeks in. In fact, it had once been a prison. One for women. There were twenty of us that lined up once we were inside and with me being at least a foot taller than the others, was made the senior of half of the group with another tall boy being the senior of the other half. We were to keep control of the others during our stay there. What a dump. Ten of us in a small dismal, filthy room that had five double bunks for us to sleep in. It only had one window that was filthy so the light had to be on even when it was daylight outside.

It definitely seemed like a prison, being woken up in the morning by the officer in charge of us, making a racket in the room and shouting out, "Hands off cocks and hands on socks" every morning at five thirty. This would give us thirty minutes to fight at the washbasins, three of them, to wash and clean our teeth before breakfast at six. Seven o'clock we would be in a class to then be shown what was expected of us.

How to make a bed navy fashion, which wasn't far off how I had been making mine for quite a few years. How to lay a table for meals, the same here too and so on. The names of a ship's interior: the floor being the deck, the ceiling a deckhead, the walls being bulkheads and many other names used aboard. The pecking order of the officers and of the stripes on their shoulders and what we had to wear when doing a daily chore and the change when we were seeing to passengers.

It was bad at first but we all got used to it and we all did well with our final tests at what we had been taught, and I got a good report from the officer that had been teaching us, rating me as excellent and top of our class. On our last day at the school, I was told that because I would then be eighteen by the time it came for me to report to a ship, I would be rated as being a steward, and would inside a week or too, know what ship I was to join and where.

I think we were all relieved to be leaving this prison to return to our homes to await our letters. Mom was pleased to see me though I wasn't sure about the man who had married her. I think he was glad that I would soon be leaving for good, little did he know that there would be times when I had ship's leave to spend there.

Though he did give me a present on my birthday, me thinking at first that he was taking the piss when I saw that it was a bible. But then he showed me how to open the inside cover that would be the ideal place to keep any money I had for if things were to be stolen on board ship, a bible would be the last thing that would be taken, and he was right. For things did tend to suddenly disappear from our cabins when in port and yet my bible was left alone. So overall, it wasn't a bad little party we had to celebrate me now being regarded as a man.

It wouldn't be long before I would learn how other men who not only played with their toys, but also what they did with them.

Seven Lucky Boys

HOT GAY EROTICA

A Compilation

DICK CLINTON

“I had to tell my close buddies how good a blow job you gave me last week in the field. I’ve been looking forward to Saturday when I was going to pick you up for another suck job, but perhaps we can all get some head today. What do ya say? After all, a good cock sucker is hard to find these days, especially one that will swallow my cum,” John continued.

“Oh man, you’re making me hot, John,” the driver Abe said.

“You mean he actually swallowed your cum? Shit, I can’t get my girl to even put her mouth on it. All she’ll do is jerk me off. I’ve never had a blow job. Can we use this cocksucker to suck us off, John?”

Then Josh, sitting next to me, grabbed his crotch and started to rub himself.

“Hey Clint, I’ve got a nice size piece of meat you can suck on right now. Why don’t you get over here and give me some head? I’m horny as a son-of-a-bitch. I’d like to see if you are as good as John says you are. Come over here, Clint, let me try out your cock sucking.”

He unbuttoned his jeans very quickly and pulled them down.

What had I gotten myself into? I was trying to figure a way to get out of this, but Abe had already left the main road and was heading down a dirt road. I was beginning to get very nervous about this whole situation. Why had John told them I was a homo? I thought that was our secret, yet the thrill of sucking some more cock intrigued me.

I looked up at John now grinning at me. Josh pulled his pants down around his hips and reached for the back of my head. His dick was thick and long. Pre-cum juices were already dripping from his big tulip shaped cock head. I slid closer to Josh so I could get his cock between my lips.

Josh was a clean-cut looking boy. I'd seen him playing football with some of the other jocks at his school. He was a popular guy and always had girls hanging around him. I'd admired his body from a distance, but never thought I would now be sucking on his big cock in front of his buddies.

He opened his shirt, exposing his rippling stomach muscles. A small hint of body fuzz was barely visible on his chest. He was partially cut but I could still pull the foreskin away from his shaft. I carefully took his cock out of his briefs, and pulled out his big hairy balls so I could lick on them. He let out a sigh then slid down in the seat so I could service his hardening cock better.

"Hey, John," Josh called out, "where you been hiding this cock sucker? Man, he knows how to handle my meat. Oh yeah. Oh, baby that feels good. Suck it down! Make that cock feel good. My God, he's taking the whole thing. Oh yeah! I've never had a blow job before. Fucken yeah! Fucken yeah!" Josh called out as I went all the way down on his big hard cock.

Josh was hot and he tasted so good. I loved the manly scent of his warm balls. He must have been playing ball today, because I could still taste the salty boy sweat on his balls.

His body started to stiffen. He put his hands on my head and started to pump his cock into my mouth. Before his climax, I caressed his strong firm chest, and pinched one nipple. I think that is what really turned him on. This boy liked his nipples played with while having his cock sucked. He started to cum. His breathing became deeper and harder. The first taste of his juicy spurt was strong, but then as he shot more cum in my mouth, it tasted better. Josh continued to pump my mouth as he came.

"Oh fuck! Oh fuck! Suck that dick, cocksucker! Shit! Take my hot load. Aw yeah! Yeah! Fuck!!!!" Josh continued to shoot load after load of cum into me.

"What a big fucken load I had. Man, that was great. Damn!" Then he laughed and held my head down on his sensitive spent cock.

I continued to lick up every drop of his young juicy sperm and milked it down to get the last few drops. John had been watching all the time and started to laugh along with Josh as he shouted out obscenities at me while I finished his load.

Abe parked the car under some trees by the side of the dirt road and turned off the motor. They both looked around at Josh now completely drained. I finished cleaning his cock from all the cum. I wiped his moist balls first with my tongue, and dried him with a clean handkerchief I had in my jeans pocket.

I lifted my head as I heard the front doors open. Abe and John were getting out of the car. Then John opened my door and motioned for me to get out.

"Okay, cock slave. Get out of the car and get on your fucking knees, cocksucker. You're gonna suck the spunk from our cocks right now…"

"YES, you are," Coach said in a commanding tone. "Your fucking hand had better be around my cock in the next few seconds or all deals are off. I will take these images to the Dean and have him deal with this situation. I am sure he will have to call your parents in and show them what their boy has been doing at school. Hell, it may have to even go before the board."

TJ could feel his heart sinking at the thought of his parents seeing him jacking off. Not to mention the Dean and the board. Fuck, he was so screwed.

"Soon everyone will know what you have been doing. How easy do you think it will be for you to land a new girl friend then? Not to mention what your teammates will think of you."

He knew it was all true. He would be the laughing stock of the school. No girls would date him. The team would tease and torment him forever. He had little choice. He would have to - have to stroke Coach. TJ's own cock jumped at the thought of touching Coach's man post.

"Now get to work on my cock!" The command in the Coach's voice left little room for argument.

Looking up at the man TJ sighed. "Is there no other way?"

"NO!" Coach said. His tone left no doubt that TJ had one option.

TJ reached up and began rubbing the thick meat through the fabric of his shorts. He could feel the heat of the swollen man meat. Feel the wetness of the pre cum on the fabric of the shorts.

"Fucking do it right," Coach ordered. "Take my fucking cock out and wrap your fingers around it and fucking stroke me properly."

TJ slowly lowered Coach's shorts and jockey briefs revealing his large man cock. It was thick and long had to be close to 2 or 3 inches longer than TJ's own cock. Not to mention thick and pre cum was leaking from the big mushroom head.

Coach let the shorts slide down his legs and to the floor. His cock throbbed as TJ finally reached out and took it in his hand. He could feel the boy's hand shake a bit as he grasp the rock hard slab of meat…

If you enjoyed this sample then look for **Coach's Private Lessons**.

WANT FREE COPIES OF MY BOOKS?

Just visit my blog and download free copies of my books:

http://chris-johns.awesomeauthors.org/

www.ingramcontent.com/pod-product-compliance
Lightning Source LLC
LaVergne TN
LVHW020651100826
845148LV00012B/2424
* 9 7 8 1 6 2 7 6 1 0 6 1 2 *